PIPPA GOODHART the lie
spider

Also by Pippa Goodhart

Flow (Shortlisted for the Smarties Prize)

Ginny's Egg

Mammoth Storybooks

Pest Friends

PIPPA GOODHART *the* lie
spider

illustrated by
RIAN HUGHES

mammoth

First published in Great Britain in 1997 by Mammoth,
an imprint of Reed International Books Limited
Michelin House, 81 Fulham Road, London SW3 6RB

ISBN 0 7497 2918 X

10 9 8 7 6 5 4 3 2

A CIP catalogue record for this book is available from the British Library

Printed in Great Britain by Cox & Wyman Ltd, Reading, Berkshire

For my Graceful Susie

'O what a tangled web we weave.

When first we practise to deceive!'

from 'Marmion' by Sir Walter Scott

Contents

1 Waking the spider   1

2 Anchoring the thread   11

3 The first thread   26

4 Spinning lies   42

5 The web takes shape   49

6 The last threads   58

7 Into the web   72

8 Trapped!   81

9 Breaking the threads   95

10 Bigger flies to trap   104

11 Jewelled threads   113

1 Waking the spider

'Mum, do you know what Andrew and that Sam Flint did to me today?'

'Not now, Izzy!' Mum was draining a steaming saucepan of carrots and peas into the sink. 'I'm trying to get tea on the table!'

'They put a sticky label on a chair with the sticky side up and made me sit on it.'

Mum opened a cupboard door with one knee, took out a bowl and poured the vegetables into it. 'That doesn't sound particularly horrible,' she said.

'It was!' said Izzy. 'It was really horrible because they wrote KICK ME on the label and it stuck on my bottom and everyone kicked me all playtime and I didn't know why.'

Mum laughed.

'It wasn't funny!' said Izzy, and she stamped her foot. 'They keep picking on me!'

'Dit-dit,' said Grace as she stood up in her highchair.

'I'll have a word with Andrew later,' said Mum. 'Now, where's your father? Tea's all ready.'

'In the garden,' said Andrew as he came in through the door.

'Tell him now!' said Izzy. 'Tell him he mustn't be horrible to me!'

'Andrew, don't be horrible to Izzy,' said Mum as she put the vegetables on the table. 'Now, call your father.'

'Dad!' shrieked Andrew.

'You didn't tell him off properly,' complained Izzy.

'Dit-dit, dit-dit!' shouted Grace, and she whacked her spoon on the tray of her highchair.

'Give Grace a biscuit, will you, Izz?'

'Can I have one too?' asked Izzy.

'No, you cannot,' said Mum. 'I'm just serving up a meal!'

'Then why can Grace have one?'

'Because I can't stand her shouting dit-dit any longer.'

Izzy opened her mouth, but Mum raised a saucepan lid in the air. 'Don't even think about trying it!' she said.

So Izzy just muttered, 'It's not fair.'

'Dit-dit!' shouted Grace. 'Dit-dit, dit-dit.' *Bang, bang, bang.*

'Just give her one,' said Mum. 'Please.'

Izzy pushed her mouth tight together and took a biscuit from the box. She slammed it down on the tray of the highchair where it broke in two. Grace stared at the broken biscuit. 'It is still a whole biscuit,' Izzy told her. 'It's just not in one piece any more.'

But Grace picked up the bits of biscuit and threw them across the floor. She screamed. Izzy covered her ears. Dad came in, crushing the biscuit to crumbs under his feet.

Mum put on her roaring lion voice. 'Sit down! Everyone!'

They did.

Mum put a heavy, hot dish of toad-in-the-hole on the table and Dad served it.

'Why is it called toad-in-the-hole when there are no toads in it and no holes?' asked Izzy.

'I don't know,' said Dad. 'Pass this to Grace, will you?'

Izzy put the plate of food in front of Grace. Grace looked at the plate, then she turned it upside down. 'No!' she screamed. 'Dit-dit! Dit-dit!'

'She still wants a biscuit,' said Izzy.

'Oh, then give her one for goodness sake,' said Mum as she sat down at the table. 'But this time don't break it!'

Izzy gave Grace an unbroken biscuit, and for a moment there was silence.

'Bliss!' sighed Mum.

'You couldn't eat real toads in holes because if they were in holes you couldn't get at them to eat,' said Izzy. 'And even if they weren't in holes nobody would eat them because they must taste toady horrible.'

'Pardon?' said Mum.

Dad looked at Mum. 'I think, Bell, that the time has come to tell them.'

'Tell who what?' asked Mum.

Dad turned to Izzy and Andrew. 'Now, children, you must be very brave. There is something about your mother that we've never told you before.'

'What?' asked Izzy, not sure whether this was a joke or serious. Was Mum ill? Or was it one of Dad's teases?

Dad answered in a solemn voice. 'The reason why you have toad-in-the-hole for your tea is – that your mother is a witch!'

Izzy and Andrew laughed.

'Oh, but I am, you know!' said Mum. She stretched out her fingers into witchy claws and put on a witchy voice. 'I've cooked toads tonight, but I sometimes use slugs and eyes of newts and toes of frogs! Didn't you know that my rice pudding is really frog spawn?' Then she sank back into being Mum again and sighed, 'I wish that I really was a witch. Then I could cast spells to make you all good and quiet and polite and . . .'

'That'd be boring,' said Andrew.

'Maybe,' said Mum. 'But I could always spell you back to being yourselves if I got bored.'

That gave Izzy an idea. 'Andrew, shall we make a book of witch spells? A spelling book! It could have the spell recipes for frogs and toads and spiders!'

'Don't be silly,' said Andrew in his big brother voice. 'Anyway, I bet you didn't know that you really can eat spiders.'

'You can't!' said Izzy.

'You can,' said Andrew. 'You can eat blue-legged tarantulas. You shove them on a stick like a kebab. You singe the hairs off them over a fire and then you cook them and eat them. They taste sort of nutty.'

Izzy screwed up her face. 'You're sort of nutty! I thought that tarantulas were poison-ous.'

'They are,' replied Andrew. 'That's why you have to pull the fangs out first before you cook them. The poison is all in the fangs. When you've finished eating you can use them like a tooth-pick to poke out any bits of spider still stuck in your teeth.'

'Can't you two find anything nicer to talk about at the meal table?' asked Dad.

'I don't believe him anyway,' said Izzy.

'I don't believe him anyway,' mimicked Andrew.

'Shut up!'

'Shut up!'

'Mum!'

'Mum!'

'Andrew! Isobel! Stop it!' said Mum. 'Or I'll use my magic to turn you both into toads and put you down a hole!'

Andrew hissed across the table to Izzy. 'It *is* true!'

'It's not!' said Izzy. 'It's a lie! Nobody would eat all those legs and eyes!'

'Pass me my book of spells!' said Mum.

'It's true!' shouted Andrew.

'Bet it's not!'

'No pudding for the next one to speak!' said Mum.

'How much do you bet?'

'Five pounds! He's lying, isn't he, Mum?'

'I don't know, and I don't care!' said Mum.

'Dit-dit,' said Grace.

'You haven't got five pounds!' said Andrew.

'Andrew!'

'I have! I've got five pounds saved for Mum's birthday.'

'Isobel!'

'All right,' said Andrew, 'you're on. I bet you five pounds that people do eat tarantula spiders.'

'Out – both of you!' said Mum.

'More dit-dit,' said Grace.

Mum looked at Dad. 'Your turn.'

Dad pointed to the door. 'You heard Mum. Out!'

'More dit-dit, more dit-dit,' said Grace.

Andrew and Izzy went. Out in the hall, Andrew poked Izzy in the ribs. 'What are you going to do about Mum's birthday now that you haven't got any money?' he asked.

'I'm not giving you any money,' said Izzy. 'I still don't believe you.'

'I'll get the book and prove it. It gives you the recipe on page seventy-one.'

Oh, bother! thought Izzy. 'Anyway, what are

you giving Mum?' she asked. 'I bet you've just got her boring chocolates or something!'

'No,' said Andrew. 'I've got her a brilliant present and it hasn't cost me anything.'

'It can't be any good then,' said Izzy. 'You are mean!' But Andrew was looking very pleased with himself and Izzy couldn't resist asking. 'What is it, anyway?'

'It's what she's always saying she wants more than anything. It's time and peace!'

'Time! How can you give someone time?' asked Izzy. 'Or peace?'

'Easy,' said Andrew. 'I've made four vouchers. Each voucher is worth one hour of me looking after Grace and you so that Mum can have the time free! Sam says he'll help me do it.'

'You want you and Sam to look after me! I don't need you to look after me! I'm nearly as old as you! And I hate Sam Flint!'

'But it's a good idea, isn't it?' said Andrew.

'No!' answered Izzy, but she knew that it was. It was a fantastic idea and Mum would love it.

There was a pause and then Andrew said, 'If

you need the money for Mum's present you don't have to pay the five pounds.'

Izzy stuck her nose in the air. 'I don't want it,' she said. 'I don't need it. I've already got Mum's present and it's much better than your stupid bits of paper!'

That was a lie.

That lie woke the Lie Spider. He was hungry. He yawned and prepared to spin a trap in which to catch himself a meal.

2 Anchoring the thread

Izzy went up to her bedroom. She slammed the door and then leaned against it.

'Bother!'

Bother Andrew, bother Mum's birthday and, most of all, bother the lie about already having a wonderful present for Mum. She hadn't got a present. Izzy pushed herself away from the door. Grace's Blue Teddy was lying on the floor. Its arms were splayed out, its glassy eyes stared, and the upside down T of its mouth grinned in a way that reminded Izzy of the expression she had just seen on Andrew's face. He knew that there was no present. Izzy kicked Blue Teddy hard. It landed in Grace's cot and grinned at her through the bars. Izzy turned her back on it and waded through the mess of Grace's toys that had flooded well over the Fairness Line. She kicked them all, soft ones, squeaky ones and hard ones, all back over the line into Grace's half of the room, and muttered, 'Stupid baby!'

Since Grace had arrived in the room two years ago, she had ruled it like a mini tyrant. Izzy was older, Izzy was wiser, but she couldn't compete with the single-mindedness of little Grace. When Grace was a tiny new baby she had kept Izzy awake by crying all night and then slept all day so that Izzy had to tiptoe quietly in her own bedroom. Mum or Dad were forever in the room feeding one end of Grace or mopping up the other, always talking endless rubbish to her.

'Who's my little curly girly? Who's my funny bunny?'

Then Grace had grown into a cot and that used up even more space than the Moses basket had. She learned to crawl and then walk and she got at everything – school books, hair, favourite toys, everything – with scrunching, sticky fingers.

If she didn't scrumple with her fingers, she shoved things into her mouth. Grace's mouth was like the back of a dustbin lorry. She shoved everything and anything into it and chewed it to pulp. Izzy did try to keep Grace in the cot cage, but Grace clutched the bars and wailed when Izzy dumped her there. Mum or Dad always came rushing and let her out again.

'Be fair, Izz. It is Grace's room as much as yours.'

But it was so *un*fair that she and Grace were in the same room at all!

When she was in that half-awake, half-asleep weekend-morning state when you can push dreams around to suit yourself, Izzy always pushed her dreams into imagining a bedroom of her own. It didn't have to be a big room, but it would have PRIVATE on the door in big letters and it would be full of secrets. In real life there just weren't enough bedrooms in their house for one each. But why couldn't she share with Andrew? Why should she, a proper school-going person, be stuck with an untamed monster baby who was nearly seven years younger than her?

There was less than two years' difference in age between Izzy and Andrew! They used to share a room when they were tiny, and it was wonderful. The games they played during the day carried on into night-time. They were best friends. Then, the summer that Izzy was three, Andrew had got his own room and started school. Izzy lost him day and night all at once. For the first time in her life she had to think and do things by herself.

Four years later, when Mum and Dad said that there was going to be a new baby, Izzy had hoped to get Andrew back with her. She supposed that Andrew would give up the little bedroom for the baby and come back to sharing the big bedroom with her. But no. Andrew was left where he was and Izzy got dumped with the baby, and found herself lumped together with her as 'the girls'. It would be, 'Tell the girls to get ready, would you, Andrew?' or 'Andrew can stay up and watch it, but it's too late for the girls.'

It made Izzy fizz with fury.

'My name is Izzy,' she would shout. 'I-Z-Z-Y. Izzy. That's my name. I am not part of a two-headed monster called The Girls. I am me! Izzy!'

'Sorry!' they would say, but they soon forgot and started referring to 'the girls' again.

A few weeks ago Izzy had made the Fairness Line down the middle of her bedroom carpet. She had glued a bright red ribbon on to the carpet to divide the room into two: the half nearest the door for Grace and the half by the window for Izzy. Then she showed it to Mum.

'You've used *glue*!' shouted Mum. 'Glue on the carpet! Oh, Izzy!'

Funny how Mum remembered her name whenever she was cross, thought Izzy.

The Fairness Line stayed because Mum said that it would leave a sticky line if they took it off, but the line didn't work. Grace didn't understand the idea of territory. She and her toys were forever over the line and, besides, half the problem with Grace was her noise and her smells and neither of those things had any idea of staying behind a line. They blasted and wafted into Izzy's space, just as they had before the line was there.

Izzy kicked the last piece of Duplo off her side of the carpet, put out her arms like Blue

Teddy, and let herself fall backwards on to her bed. Then she stared up at the ceiling. It was plain white. Like paper. Blank. One day I'll paint it blue like the sky, thought Izzy. I'll paint clouds and birds and butterflies and aeroplanes on it and perhaps some very tiny fairies that are too small for Andrew to notice. I could buy some of those star-shaped stickers that glow in the dark. I could . . . But those thoughts weren't helping with the Mum present problem. Izzy flipped over on to her tummy and scrunched her eyes so tightly shut that she began to feel dizzy. Think. What would Mum like most if she could have anything? Nothing boring like getting the glue off the carpet. Something special! Something valuable! Something to wipe out Andrew's big brother sneers and make him realise that Izzy was worth being friends with again! What could do all that?

Izzy pictured Mum in her mind. Good old ordinary Mum. Not thin, not fat. Ordinary brown hair that wasn't very long or very short. Ordinary jeans and jumpers like most of the other mothers. Nice comfortable Mum. Mum was one of 'the mums' just as Izzy had become one of 'the girls'.

I wonder if sometimes Mum wants her own name and wants to look different? Izzy thought. I would if I was her. I'd like to make people look at me once in a while. Sparkling jewels would do it. Perhaps a diamond necklace spelling out 'Bell', Mum's name? That would be a wonderful present, but impossible. Jewels cost far too much money. Even Dad couldn't afford to buy her that. No. Think again, Izz.

Izzy sat up and tried to think sensibly this time. Andrew had thought of a brilliant present that didn't cost anything. Time and peace were things that Mum was always wanting, but what else did she wish for? She often longed for an extra pair of hands.

'Yes!' said Izzy, leaping off the bed. That would do. She could easily make an extra pair of hands! She opened the bedroom door and shouted down the stairs, 'Mum! Are there any old gloves that I can have, please?'

Mum's head peered up the stairs.

'Gloves! Whatever for?'

'Just something,' said Izzy.

'Well I think there might be some odd ones

in the box under the stairs. We've lost the pair to one of Grace's yellow mittens and one of Dad's green gloves is full of holes. You're welcome to have them if you like.'

'Thanks!'

Izzy leaped down the stairs and began rummaging. All she had to do was stuff the old gloves and sew them on to Mum's coat. Then Mum could use her real hands for carrying shopping while Grace held on to a stuffed one. Brilliant! The other stuffed hand could be ready in case they ever did get the dog that Izzy wanted. Then they could tie the dog's lead to the glove and Mum could take the dog for a walk at the same time as taking Grace shopping and it would be hardly any extra trouble.

Izzy found the green and yellow gloves, one tiny and one huge, and she suddenly knew that it wasn't a brilliant idea after all. The gloves looked silly and they would look even more silly hanging off Mum's coat. Andrew would laugh and say that her idea was stupid, in that voice of his. Perhaps rubber gloves would work? Pink ones would look almost like real hands, but then

Izzy thought of Grace and knew that wouldn't work either. Grace, who wouldn't eat a biscuit unless it was a perfect one, would never agree to holding a clammy rubber hand instead of a real, live, Mum one. Izzy threw the gloves back into the box. Bother! She stomped back upstairs and slammed into her room. Grace was there now. She was holding her baby doll by its hair and feeding it a plastic banana. Izzy took hold of the long curtains by her bed. She pulled them away from the window and over her bed, then tucked them under the mattress on the room side so that they made a tent. Mum didn't like her doing that.

'It'll bring the curtain rail down if you go on pulling at the curtains like that!' But she hadn't actually banned Izzy from doing it.

Izzy liked the curtains. She had chosen the material at the market. It had bright, busy flowers all over. She climbed into her curtain tent and sat cross-legged in the cosy dimness with the curtain flowers glowing from the light behind them. She heard Mum's feet on the stairs.

'Bath-time, Gracie.'

'No,' said Grace.

'Yes,' said Mum.

'No way.'

'Yes way. Remember I'm a witch! I'm going to chase you and put you into my bubbling cauldron!'

And Grace went off, squealing and happy.

Mum deserves a special present, thought Izzy, but what could it be? She twisted round and saw herself in the window glass. The darkness outside had turned the window into a mirror. Izzy cupped her hands on either side of her face and pushed it up against the cold, hard glass. It was strange how you had to make it dark on your side of the window if you wanted to get past the mirror and see through to the other side. Izzy looked out at the garden, all black and white and grey in the slight light that leaked out from the houses round about. The garden looked sad. There were still a few last pansies, but most of the flowers had shrivelled and drooped and given up trying now that summer was cooling away. There was the old apple tree with the swing and, in front of it, the lawn. The lawn was scuffed by bikes and football.

Mum always said that once the children were older she was going to make the garden really nice. Now there was a thought! Would Mum like something for the garden as her present? Izzy pushed her face, squashing her nose white against the glass, and looked for ideas. The lawn was the dullest, scruffiest bit of the garden and September was the right time of year for planting bulbs. That could be good, thought Izzy. Lots of bulbs! Bulbs planted in a special pattern – writing 'I love Mum' across the whole lawn! Mum would have to wait until the Spring before the crocuses and daffodils came up and she could properly see her present, but that didn't matter. In fact it made it better! Mum once said that Izzy was the best birthday present she had ever had. That was because Izzy had been born on Mum's thirtieth birthday. It was a nice thing to say, but it had always worried Izzy that Mum thought she had already had the best present she would ever get. Fancy feeling the best was already over! Each year Izzy knew that the bookmark she made or the bubble bath she bought were poor presents compared with having a baby. But when Mum planted seeds and grew things to put in the garden, she called the plants her babies. And the bulbs would be like babies, because you have to wait for them to come and then you watch them live and grow, but without any nappies and sick and mess. Perfect! Izzy sat back so that she saw herself and not the garden in the window mirror. She smiled. All she had to do now was find the money to buy hundreds of bulbs.

'Your go in the bath now, Izz,' said Mum, coming in with Grace wrapped in a towel.

Izzy climbed out from her bed tent and Mum looked at her.

'What are you looking so pleased about?'

'Something to do with birthdays,' smiled Izzy.

'Well, don't get so fizzed up about your birthday. You'll make yourself ill!' laughed Mum. 'You did that when you were four. You got into such a state you missed out on your own party!'

'That was ages ago. And anyway, it's to do with your birthday, not mine!'

In the bath Izzy thought about money for buying bulbs. She had the five pounds, but that was promised to Andrew. She could probably get this week's pocket money early if she told Dad it was for Mum's present. But then what? She would need more than that to make a really good display. In old-fashioned books girls got money by selling their chestnut tresses of hair to a wig-maker. Izzy's hair wasn't chestnut-coloured, it was mouse-coloured and it was only just long enough to scrape into a ponytail for school. Izzy lay back in the bath and trapped a bubble of air under her flannel, pulled it down into the water and then slowly squashed the bubbles out of it. She wished that she could bubble out ideas like that. She was about to squash out more bubbles when she noticed that the bathroom window was steamed up, and that gave her an idea. I'll try a window wish, she decided.

Izzy pulled herself out of the comfortable warmth of the bath and stepped on to the mat. She took a towel from the rail and cloaked it round herself, and then went dripping over to the window. Izzy hadn't done a window wish for years, but you never quite knew about magic. She lifted a finger up like a wand pencil and wrote in the window's mist: *Mum's present*. There was just enough room, so she added a small, *Please*. Then she levered the handle and pushed open the window.

The last time Izzy had window-wished had been a horrible foggy day soon after baby Grace moved into her room. Izzy had drawn a big house on the bedroom window, but the picture wish had not been taken. It had stayed on the window for days and dribbled until Izzy couldn't bear it any longer and wiped it off with her sleeve. She supposed that the wish hadn't been taken because it was too greedy. A new house was a big thing to ask for. She also began to think that perhaps Andrew was right and that wishes didn't work anyway. But now she smiled as the chilly breeze from outside slowly took the message about Mum's present, leaving the window blank once more. Perhaps this one really was being carried on the breeze, off to wherever wishes are granted?

Lie Spider watched. He shuddered at the thought of the lie being turned into truth, but he knew that wishing couldn't do that. He knew that there would soon be more lies. Lie Spider secured the end of his thread and waited.

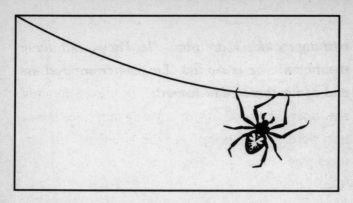

3 The first thread

The next day, after school, Izzy cleaned the car and sorted all the jigsaw pieces into the right boxes. Those jobs earned her three pounds fifty towards Mum's present. Then, suddenly, the window wish came true.

Mum turned from the sink and asked, 'Would you be a kind Izz and empty the waste-paper bins and put out the dustbin?'

'How much will you pay me?'

Mum sighed.

'It is for your birthday present,' said Izzy.

'Well, twenty-five pence, then. But it doesn't count as being kind if you ask for money!'

Izzy couldn't afford to be kind in the next

26

two days if she was to have any hope of buying the bulbs. She collected the bins from upstairs and downstairs. Outside in the grey evening chill she opened the dustbin, turning her face away and holding her breath as the smell of old cat-food tins leaped up. Then she let the breath go, 'Oh!'

Izzy dropped the bins she was holding and she gazed down into the dark, dingy depths of the dustbin. There, magically untouched by the old toothpaste tube or the rusty-coloured splodges of tinned spaghetti, was a flash of bright white with Izzy's name printed on it in clear dark letters.

Ms Isobel Bonnet

A shiver ran down Izzy's spine. Who would leave a message for her in a dustbin? Could it be one of Sam Flint's horrible tricks? He and Andrew might have put it there on purpose and hidden something really slimy and smelly under it. But how could they have known that Izzy would do the bins? No, it couldn't be them. But, if it wasn't them, then it felt spookily like magic. Izzy felt a fizz of excitement in her tummy as she rose up on tiptoe and reached carefully down into the smelly dustbin. She pulled out the paper with her name on it and held it up to the light. It was an envelope and there was more on it than just her name. There was a picture showing a woman with lots of very blonde hair. She was wearing a red bikini and sitting on a very yellow beach under a bright blue sky. The woman sat in an L shape and Izzy's name and address were in front of her face. She had her head thrown back and she was laughing. The laugh showed lots of white teeth and one of them had a tiny white star on the corner of it to make it look extra shiny. There were little white stars on something else too. The woman was wearing lots of jewellery. She had earrings, necklaces, bracelets and rings, all glittering gold and silver, red and blue. The jewellery looked strange with the swimming costume. There was more writing under her bottom. It said:

Claim your free jewels for a sparkling future!

Claim your jewels! *Free* jewels! Could there possibly be jewels for Mum's birthday after all? Izzy turned the envelope over. There was more writing on the back:

You can win £150,000!
Just think of the new dream home,
the exotic holiday or the fabulous new car
that could be yours!
Claim your prize within ten days and
double your win to £300,000!
Send off today and double your dreams!

Izzy's mouth dropped open. With all that money they could have a big new house with lots of bedrooms! And a big garden! Then Izzy frowned and chewed at her bottom lip. It was almost too much. It was impossible! What sort of power could remember and make a two-year-old, dribbled window wish come true as well as the present wish? It was frightening to think that some 'thing' knew her mind and thoughts so well, and had such power that it could make the impossible happen. Izzy held the envelope reverently and closed her eyes for a moment just to test if it was real. When she opened her eyes, the envelope, the picture and the writing were all still there and she noticed something else. Across the corner of the envelope it said:

Your winning numbers are enclosed!

Winning numbers! *Winning*! Izzy felt a bit sick, a bit dizzy. Was the 'thing' watching her now and reading her mind? She wanted to get back to the warmth and light of her bedroom. She quickly stuffed the fallen rubbish into the dustbin and wheeled it out on to the pavement. Then she grabbed the empty bins and raced back into the house and up the stairs.

'I'll just get my purse and give you that twenty-five pence,' called her mother, but Izzy didn't want pennies now.

'That's all right. I don't think that you should have to pay me to do the bins after all!'

Izzy's mother raised her eyebrows and put her purse away.

Upstairs there were sounds of Dad giving

Grace her bath. As usual, time alone in the bedroom would be short. Izzy firmly shut the door and threw herself down on to her bed. Then she looked at the wish-answering envelope. It was plump-full of paper. She pushed a thumb under the flap and levered, tearing up and down until she could tip out the envelope's contents on to the bed. Out came what Mum would call bumph. There were scratchcards and letters and pictures and envelopes. Izzy picked up what seemed to be the main letter. Would it be signed by the 'thing'? By the fairies or God or Father Christmas? Who *did* grant wishes? If Andrew were here he would say, 'Don't be stupid, Izz. There has to be some logical explanation.'

For a moment Izzy was tempted to show the letter to Andrew, but then she suddenly saw the logical explanation for herself. It was there in front of her.

Ms Isobel Bonnet

That's what it said: 'Ms'. Izzy pushed her hair

behind her ears and crossed her legs. Good. She didn't need Andrew to tell her. Ms meant Mrs or Miss or any sort of female. The Ms on this envelope would be meaning Mrs. It was meant for Mum. Mum was an Isobel too. Izzy had been named after her because of being born on Mum's birthday. Most people called Mum Mrs Bonnet or Bell and a lot of people didn't even know that she was really called Isobel, but she was. Izzy was mostly called Izzy or Izz or Fizzy Izz, but she was an Isobel too. So this bumph was being sent to Mum. That was a relief, and it didn't have to spoil things. She might not be the Isobel that the bumph people meant when they addressed the envelope, but Izzy still *was* Ms Isobel Bonnet! They would have to give her any prizes that they promised to a Ms Isobel Bonnet at that address! Who were they anyway? Izzy looked at the bottom of the letter. It was signed by Mr Tom Bottomly of Underwear World. It had been sent by a knicker-seller called Bottomly! Izzy rolled on to her back and read:

Congratulations!
You, Ms Bonnet, have luck smiling upon
you. Our special selection computer chose
to send good fortune in the direction of
Leicester. It homed in on Daisy Road and
picked the Bonnet household to shower
with its bountiful cornucopia of prizes.

What was a cornucopia? Never mind, it sounded like lots of prizes. Izzy read on:

You have already successfully completed
the first two rounds in our SuperDraw!

Brilliant! So she was well on the way to getting a prize, and Mum must have started doing the competition if she had already got through two rounds! Mum, who said you had to earn anything you wanted in life, had sneakily gone in for the competition! And she must have meant to carry on with it when she was doing so well. She must have thrown the envelope away by mistake. Should she give it back to Mum? No, Izzy decided. After all, if I win the competition I'll be giving the money to Mum anyway, so it comes to the same thing. Izzy pushed her hair back behind her ears and read on.

> *Six numbers have been allocated to you personally, Ms Bonnet. Any one of those numbers could win you £150,000 that could make your dreams come true! Open the golden lucky number envelope now and match your lucky numbers with the winning number: 7524237.*

Wow! Izzy picked up the golden envelope. She held her breath and drew out a scratchcard with six places to rub away some silver stuff and find lucky numbers underneath. Izzy pushed at it with her thumbnail and uncovered the first of her lucky numbers – 7534237. Nearly the same! But nearly right was no better than being completely wrong. The second and third numbers were near misses as well, but then . . .

'Yes!'

Number four matched exactly! Did that mean

that the money was hers for definite? Izzy picked up the letter again.

If you, Ms Bonnet, are fortunate enough to find a matching number, then you are entitled to enter the very final draw. In fact the winning number has already been drawn! Yes, you could already be that winner! Simply return your lucky number in the envelope marked 'Yes, Please!' and we will let you know which prize you have won because, yes! you have won a prize! Whether or not you, Ms Bonnet, are the winner of our £150,000 top prize, you are guaranteed a treasure-trove of prizes! A collection of precious stones – genuine diamonds, sapphires and rubies – awaits in a velvet pochette labelled with your name. Claim it and it is yours!

A bagful of jewels! With her name on it! Just waiting to be claimed! It was perfect. Mum would sparkle at last.

When Mum and Dad got engaged Dad had

been too poor to buy diamonds. He had gone to evening classes and made Mum a home-made ring using a stone which they had found on their first walk together. It was a funny little pebble – see-through and with a tiny, deep-green mossy frond trapped inside it. Dad said the stone was called moss agate and that the ferny plant had been alive millions of years ago. It was interesting but it didn't sparkle. It wasn't a proper engagement ring and Izzy felt sad about that. And now she could put it right. She would give Mum not just one diamond, but a whole bagful of starry diamonds, rose-red rubies and sapphires as blue as the sky! And on top of that she might get £150,000 or even £300,000 if she sent the envelope off in time!

So, thought Izzy, how do I get the jewels and money? She could hear Dad coming along the landing with a giggling Grace. Bloomin' Grace! Izzy stuffed all the paper bits and pieces under the duvet and tried to make her face look normal.

'Will you open the door, Izz?' called Dad. 'I haven't got any hands.'

'Yes, but don't let Grace look in my bed!'

'OK.'

Izzy opened the door to let Dad fly Grace into the room. Grace had a towel under her arms and Dad held the two ends together above her curly blonde head. Grace flapped her arm wings and kicked her tail legs.

'You look a busy Izzy – what are you up to?' asked Dad as he lowered Grace to the floor and opened a drawer to look for pyjamas.

'Just something for Mum's birthday,' said Izzy. 'It's secret.'

'Do you need any help with it?' asked Dad. He tried to lasso Grace with the neck of a pyjama top. Grace was climbing on to Izzy's bed and lifting a corner of the duvet. Izzy slapped the duvet back down.

'Get out of it, Grace!' Then she turned to Dad. 'What I need is some time and some peace from her!'

Dad laughed.

'You sound just like your mother!'

Grace squealed happily as Dad hung her upside down by her ankles. 'You can use my study for half an hour, if that would help.'

'Thanks!' said Izzy. If she won the money, then she would buy Dad a brand-new car – a fast, red one!

Izzy took the bumph out of her bed and hid it under her jumper. Then she went downstairs to the study. The study was chilly and dark. Izzy clicked on the light. It was a small room crammed full of Dad. There was a Dad smell, there were his work books and files and his drawing-board and the computer and his dried-up old paints that he was going to get out and use one of these days. There was a tatty old desk and one chair. It was an old chair that Grandpa had given Dad years ago. It had a wide bottom that sank down where the wickerwork had sagged, and smooth, wooden arms that came forward and then down. Izzy thought the chair was like Grandpa – a cross old man with his hands on his knees. But it was friendly-cross and Izzy liked to sit on its big lap. She sat down now and plonked the pile of bumph on to the desk in front of her. What had she got to do? Oh, yes, put the confirmation of entry into the Yes, Please! envelope. Izzy checked through the instructions again, kissed the matching lucky number and pushed it and the claim for the jewels into the pink envelope.

There were photographs on the back of the envelope. They showed two women. There was Mrs X from Kent in black and white, who had her head in her hands. Mrs X hadn't sent her lucky number in on time and had missed doubling her prize. Mrs B. Cook from Cheshire was in colour and smiling. She had won the full £300,000 by sending in her entry on time!

When was 'on time'? Izzy looked back at the letter. It was dated 10th September, so to get it there within ten days it should arrive by the 20th. Good. Mum's birthday was on the 21st so there was just time for the jewels to arrive by the promised return of post. Then Izzy froze. September 20th was Friday! September 20th was tomorrow! Izzy looked at her watch. Nearly eight o'clock. There was no way the post was going to get the pink Yes, please! envelope to the prize place in time. Izzy put her head in her hands. I must look just like Mrs X, she thought. The wishing luck had brought her so close. She mustn't let it run out now.

'Think,' said Izzy. She knocked on her head with her knuckles. 'Think.'

All that was needed was to get the silly envelope to the place by tomorrow. There must be a way to do it! A motorbike courier would cost too much. She didn't have a pigeon. Think again.

Izzy looked at the address printed on the envelope:

Underwear World
P.O. Box 45
Leicester

Leicester! Of all the places in the country, in the world, in the universe that Underwear World might have been, they were in Leicester! Izzy looked up to the ceiling.

'Thank you!'

She looked at her reflection on Dad's blank computer screen.

'Take it there yourself, Ms Isobel Bonnet.'

It might be fun.

Lie Spider read the promise of real jewels and smiled. Truth can be wrapped and given in such a way that it is received as something different. Truth can be made to lie. Lie Spider spun the first strong thread and secured it. His web was begun.

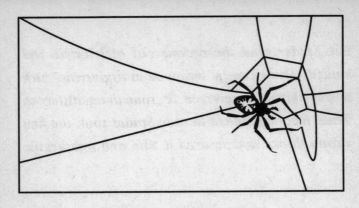

4 Spinning lies

Upstairs, Grace was asleep in her cot, arms flung upwards in a stick-'em-up position, head on one side and small snores puffing from her mouth. Izzy looked at her. *Snore, puff, snore, puff.* I wonder if she's dreaming? Do two-year-olds dream? They certainly had nightmares. Izzy could remember the sick freezing terror the night she was eaten by a tiger when she was about Grace's age. Andrew had roared to frighten the tiger away. Grace should have somebody to shoo her nightmares away for her, thought Izzy. I suppose it should be me. She bent down and kissed her little sister's sleeping head.

'Goodnight, you,' she said.

Then Izzy swung her schoolbag up from the

floor and tipped everything out of it on to her bed. What was she going to need tomorrow? Not books or the pencil-case. Perhaps something to wear? Izzy pulled out a drawer and took out the yellow knobbly jumper that Nan had knitted for her. It was her lucky jumper. She had been wearing it on the day she'd won something on a bottle stall and knocked down a coconut *and* won a goldfish by throwing Ping-Pong balls into jamjars, all in one afternoon. She could swap her school sweat-shirt for the lucky jumper once she'd left home, then she wouldn't be labelled with Overdale Junior School if any busybody wanted to report a schoolgirl not at school.

The jumper almost filled the bag. Izzy opened the side pockets and put her purse in one side and the Leicester *A-Z* in the other. She had found Underwear World in the telephone directory. Its address was Union Lane, down by the canal. She would use the *A-Z* map to show her how to get there from the bus station. The purse contained the three pounds fifty that Izzy had earned and the five pounds that Andrew hadn't yet asked for. That should be plenty for a couple of bus rides.

Izzy looked at the pile of bumph. She wouldn't need all of it. As well as the envelopes and scratchcards and things, there was a catalogue of pants and bras and nighties and bathing costumes. Izzy opened it at a page full of socks. There were teeny-tiny pink and blue socks for babies, boring grey and blue school socks, funny stripy, spotty and picture socks. There were even socks with pictures of pop stars on them. Did famous people really want to wrap around smelly feet?

'Stupid!' muttered Izzy, and she threw the catalogue into the bin.

'Stoopid,' echoed a small, sleepy voice.

'Grace! How long have you been awake?'

Grace stood up in her cot with her arms dangling over the top rail. She smiled sleepily at Izzy and pointed to the bed.

'Izzy backpack,' she said.

'Yes,' whispered Izzy. 'I'm not going to school tomorrow. I'm going on a treasure hunt for jewels!'

Why am I telling her? wondered Izzy. But Grace wouldn't understand and couldn't tell and it was a relief to have told one member of the family what she was doing.

'Just sometimes it's nice having you in my room,' she told Grace. 'Now lie down!'

Grace lay down and Izzy tickled her through the cot bars until she giggled and squirmed.

'Do it again!'

'No, that's enough. Time for sleep.'

'Do it again! Do it again!'

But Grace was half asleep already and, as Izzy pulled the covers up, Grace curled up on to one side and closed her eyes as she muttered one last sleepy, 'Do it again.'

As she undressed ready for bed, Izzy thought about tomorrow. Going into town alone would be an adventure. She had never planned and done anything adventurous on her own before. It had always been shared with Andrew, always with Andrew leading. One summer, years ago, Andrew had found out that Australia was on the other side of the world, and so they had decided to dig a tunnel from their garden to Australia.

The two of them had planned and worked in secret, taking it in turns to dig at the soft, sandy earth behind the shed with a sandpit spade while the other watched out for Mum. They didn't actually get to Australia. They only dug about a metre of the way, but it didn't seem to matter. It was fun to try and, as Andrew said, you could always go to a zoo to see a kangaroo. They were a good team in those days, Andrew and Izzy. They knew just how each other thought and felt. Sometimes they still did. Izzy had the uncomfortable feeling that Andrew knew now that she was up to something. She had better plan tomorrow carefully.

Izzy tore a bit of paper from her writing-pad and sat cross-legged on her bed. She chewed at her pencil, then wrote:

1. *Leave the house without anybody guessing anything.*
2. *Try to walk with Andrew so that he runs on to school without me.*
3. *Look all around and make sure that*

nobody can see, then turn left at bottom of road.

Left took you to the bus stop. Right took you to the school.

4. *Hide in playground bushes. Put on Nan's jumper and change hair.*

5. *Go to bus stop and get on bus. If anybody asks, say you are going to the dentist.*

6. *Get off bus. Walk to Underwear World and post letter.*

7. *Back to bus station and get bus back to school.*

8. *Tell Mr Clarke you've been to dentist.*

Izzy pulled at a drawer and took out a crumpled sticker with a toothy-grin picture on it. It would make her story really convincing if she wore the sticker into school. And that was it – all sorted! Izzy hugged her knees to her chest, smug with her plan.

When she reached out to close her bedroom curtains for the night she could see stars.

'*Twinkle, twinkle little star*,' sang Izzy very quietly. '*How I wonder what you are. Up above the world so high, Like a diamond in the sky . . .*'

Tonight's stars really were like diamonds scattered on dark blue velvet.

'*When you wish upon a star, Makes no difference who you are . . .*'

Stars were magical. They straddled worlds and time. Stars didn't change. You could rely on them, like diamonds. 'Diamonds are for ever,' is what the advertisements said. And soon Mum would sparkle with jewels like the sky. Izzy snuggled down and pushed her thoughts off into a happy dream about Mum opening her present on her birthday morning.

Even objects with no thought to either lie or tell the truth can deceive. The light from stars deep in space can take many, many years to travel to earth. Where we see a star shining brightly in our sky, there may no longer be a star. It might be a lie. Lie Spider spun.

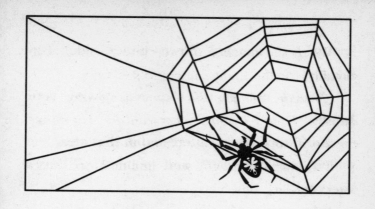

5 The web takes shape

Izzy woke next morning, her tummy churning with a mixture of cold doubt and fizzing excitement. Today already had a strange, slightly dangerous feel to it, like riding in a car with no seat belt on. Today would be the first time that Izzy had gone anywhere without an adult knowing where she was.

'You'll be free!' she told herself.

Grace was doing what she called 'dressing my 'elf'. You had to let Grace try and dress herself for a few minutes before she would let anybody help her. Just now she was pulling a pair of tights on to her head so that the two green, spotty legs dangled down either side. Izzy laughed.

'You've got plaits!' she said. 'Swing your head!'

But Grace wasn't interested in that idea. She pulled the tights off and pointed to Izzy's backpack.

'Me come too!'

'Not today,' Izzy told her. 'When you're bigger we'll do adventures together. But I've got to do today's one by my 'elf.'

Downstairs, the usual morning rush was on. Mum was slapping sandwiches together and tripping over Dad, who was polishing his shoes in the middle of the kitchen floor. Mum glanced at the clock and then at Izzy.

'Shoes,' she said. 'And do something with your hair – it looks like a haystack. Friday – have you got your library book? Don't forget to give Mr Clarke the note about Parents' Evening. Shall I put it in your bag?' Mum reached for Izzy's backpack.

'No thanks.' Izzy snatched it away. 'It's all right. I'll put it in.'

Andrew looked at her. 'You're hiding something.'

'I'm not!' said Izzy, but she couldn't look him in the eye as she said it. Part one of her plan – leaving the house without anyone guessing anything – might be tricky.

When Mum said goodbye to Izzy on the doorstep ten minutes later, Izzy hugged her tight.

'You look all excited,' said Mum. 'Have you got something special happening at school today?'

'No,' said Izzy. She hadn't – not at school.

Mum pushed Izzy gently away.

'Well, you'd better get off to school, special or not! Bye, Izzpot!' and she closed the door.

That was good. Mum wasn't bothered about her. So why did it hurt that Mum had pushed her and closed the door on her?

Izzy swung her bag on to her back, took a deep breath, and walked out through the front gate. There, she'd done it. She'd successfully completed part one of her plan.

As she walked down the road towards school, Izzy thought about part two:

> *2. Try to walk with Andrew so that he runs on to school without me.*

She looked around, but she couldn't see Andrew. He should be just a little further down the road, but he wasn't. Sam Flint was, and Andrew normally walked with him. Izzy ran to catch up with Sam.

'Where's Andrew?'

'Don't know.'

'Will you give him a message? Please?'

Sam was in the same class as Andrew. 'OK,' he said.

'Tell him that I've got something for him and I'll give it to him in the playground at lunchtime!'

'OK,' said Sam again, and Izzy let him walk on ahead.

Izzy skipped a couple of steps, then pulled out her plan.

> *3. Look all around and make sure that nobody can see, then turn left at bottom of road.*

4. Hide in playground bushes. Put on Nan's jumper and change hair.

By the time Izzy had reached the bottom of Daisy Road, her heart was galloping. Calm down, Izz, she told herself. Act normal.

The little playground was empty. Izzy bobbed down and hunched her way through some bushes into the small open space behind. It used to be Andrew's and her den when Mum brought them here years ago. It seemed to have shrunk since then, but there was just enough room for her. Izzy swapped Nan's yellow jumper for her school sweat-shirt, then pulled out the elastic holding her ponytail together. She brushed and retied her hair into high-up bunches that hung like spaniel ears down each side of her head. Then she pushed her fringe back off her forehead and held it there with a hairband. She repacked her bag and crept back out into the playground. Now for part five – getting on to the bus.

Izzy kept still and quiet at the bus stop so that she wouldn't be noticed. You didn't have to be invisible to be invisible, just still and quiet and blending in with the colours. Izzy glanced down at her bright yellow jumper. It did blend quite well with the ladies' umbrellas and bright anoraks but not with the dark uniforms of the big school-children. Well, she wasn't a schoolchild today. What am I, then? wondered Izzy, but a bus was arriving and she didn't have time to answer herself.

The bus driver gave her a long look as she stepped aboard.

'A return to the central bus station, please,' she said.

'Half fare?'

'Yes, please.'

'Shouldn't you be at school?'

Izzy glowed hot inside. She hoped that it didn't show.

'I'm going to the dentist,' she said.

'Sooner you than me!' said the driver, and he punched buttons and a ticket and change swirled into the bowl.

Izzy went upstairs and had the whole front seat to herself. She loved the way the bus roared and rumbled and swayed along, high above the normal world. It must have felt a bit like that for people years ago when they travelled in big ships with roaring engines, as they tossed through the sea, away from their homelands to a new life in Africa or Australia or America.

She could see the top of Kirsty's head as she hurried to school. That was Izzy's homeland, down there with the other Overdale Junior School children. Then the bus lurched round a corner. Friends and school were left behind and Izzy was surprised to feel sad. That was silly. She should be feeling excited, adventurous. Think of the prizes, she told herself. Jewels for Mum! You're on a pirate ship, off to win treasure to bring home to your loved ones. There might even be enough treasure to buy a big new house! Think of the house. Choose one now. Izzy looked down. The houses looked like doll's-houses arranged on a shelf in some giant supermarket. Most of them were like home in Daisy Road in symmetrical, semi-detached pairs with bay windows bulging like toad eyes at the front. But there was one house that was different. It was older and bigger and set back from the road.

There was a dog running through long grass in the big garden. If a house like that fits a dog like that, then that's what I want, thought Izzy.

She was about to turn back to face forwards when a sudden flash of movement at the back of the bus caught her interest. Which of the passengers had moved? Rows of bored faces looked blankly back at her. Up in the top corner of the bus there was a mirror. It was round and curved and if you leaned forward and squinted up at it you could see everyone on the top deck of the bus squashed and squeezed to fit into its circle. It showed the same dull people stacked in rows, but now they were bulged and compressed into interesting alien beings. The man in the grey suit with big ears has a cloning-machine in his briefcase, Izzy decided, and that is why the man next to him looks almost identical to him. Who will he clone next? Then an icy finger seemed to zip down Izzy's back and freeze her stomach. There, squashed and distorted like the others and sitting at the back of the bus was Izzy Bonnet. *She* had been cloned! No she hadn't. It wasn't her face after all. It was Andrew's. Andrew was following her!

Everyone knows that words can lie, but appearance can lie too. Izzy had used both. Lie Spider completed his framework of spokes and began to spin and stick, netting the web, spiralling around and around.

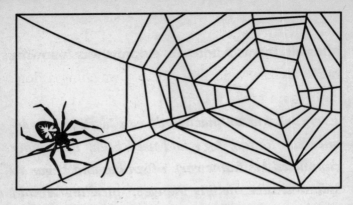

6 The last threads

Andrew moved to sit beside Izzy at the front of the bus. Aware that the rows of faces behind were no longer so bored, Izzy whispered as she tried to explain to him what she was doing. Andrew nearly forgot to whisper back.

'Jewels! Blimey, Izz, you'd believe anything!'

'I wouldn't!'

'You would. Do you remember when Sam and I told you that the Queen wipes her bottom on five-pound notes? You believed that!'

'I did not!' whispered Izzy back.

'You did! You told Dad about it!'

'I was just tricking him like you'd tricked me!' But she had believed it. It was horrible when she found out that they had lied to her. 'Anyway,' she said, 'you've believed stupid things too. You were the one who thought that waggling a dog's tail would make it happy.'

'That was different.'

'How?'

'Because that wasn't believing something I'd been told. It was inventing an idea that should have worked. If dogs wag their tails when they're happy then it makes sense that it should make them happy if you wag their tails.'

'It didn't though, did it?' Izzy held up the thumb with the shiny smooth scar where the Alsatian had bitten her. 'And if you really thought it would work, then why did you make me be the one to try it out?'

'Oh, I'm not going into all that again!' said Andrew. 'But seriously, Izz, nobody is going to give away *real* jewels. You must have got that wrong!'

'It says "genuine diamonds, sapphires and rubies". Look!'

Andrew looked. 'Then they must want something in return or why would they do it?'

'There was a catalogue of swimming costumes

and socks and things and I think they hope that you'll buy some, but you don't have to.'

'Are you sure?'

'Yes I am. And if you don't want to be part of it then you can just go back to school. I didn't ask you to come, did I? You sneaked after me.'

'I had to.'

'Why?'

'Because I couldn't let you go off on your own with nobody knowing where you were. You're only nine.'

'Ten tomorrow! And anyway, it's none of your business. You just wanted to find out what I was getting for Mum's birthday.'

'I did not! I wanted to keep you out of trouble. It's against the law not to go to school.' Izzy had known that, but she had forgotten. She didn't feel as if she was breaking any law. She didn't feel wicked.

'Well, you aren't at school either!' Izzy paused. 'Are we really in trouble with the police?'

'I think it would be Mum and Dad who get into trouble.'

'But that's not fair! They don't even know that we're not at school.'

'So we should go back now before anything happens.'

'No,' said Izzy.

'What do you mean, no?'

'I mean no, I'm not going back until I've delivered the letter. I'll miss out on the chance for the bonus prize if it isn't delivered today and it won't even take long.'

The bus was turning into the bus station. Izzy took hold of Andrew's arm.

'You come too. It'll be fun! And then we'll go back quick, I promise. The jewels and money can be from you too, if you like.'

Andrew sighed.

'Oh, all right. I suppose a little longer won't make much difference now that we've missed registration.'

Walking towards Union Lane with Andrew reading the *A-Z* map made Izzy feel part of the old partnership again. It was nice.

'Hey,' she said, 'do you remember when we

tried digging a tunnel to the other side of the world?'

'Yes, and you put biscuits and bananas and things in a bag . . .'

'They were to eat on the walk to Australia . . .'

' . . . and Mum found them weeks later, all mouldy and smelly! You know, I really thought we would get there.'

'Me too.'

'Have you got any bananas and biscuits today?' Andrew pointed to her backpack.

'There might be. I didn't see what Mum put in my lunch.'

They walked companionably past the shops and down into the stale, damp air of the subway.

Izzy moved closer to Andrew.

'I'm glad you came,' she told him.

They walked down past big office blocks and away from the main roads to an older part of town with the canal running through it.

Turning into Union Lane was like stepping through a time warp into a past age. The lane was narrow. On either side of it were tall Victorian factories made of red brick, with rows of small-paned windows. The lane was so narrow and the buildings so tall that the whole place was in shadow. It was colder than the roads they had come from and there were no sounds of nearby cars or people. The only noise from the lane itself was a strange clicking and humming from inside the buildings.

Izzy looked up. Through some of the windows she could see cone-shaped bobbins of coloured thread impaled on metal spikes, dancing a jerky dance as machines behind the windows grabbed for more thread. In her mind, urchins in caps and clogs and ragged old clothes were working at the knitting-machines or stitching buttonholes.

'There you are,' said Andrew. 'Underwear World. That's what you want, isn't it?'

Underwear World was at the end of the lane and some effort had gone into making that building look more modern. A big plastic sign said UNDERWEAR WORLD at an angle up the wall, as if it had glooped out of some giant toothpaste tube. Under the sign was a window and a door. Behind the big plain-glass window was a display of plastic people wearing underwear and swimming costumes. There was a tall plastic woman who looked at Izzy out of eyes embedded in bruise-coloured make-up. She had long fingers and a long neck and she was wearing tiny lacy triangles on her shiny hard bosom and bottom.

Andrew pointed to the lacy pants and bra. 'See that?' he asked. 'Did you know that you can make clothes out of spiders' webs? Queen Victoria had a dress made from them.'

'Really?'

'Yep. A Chinese ambassador gave it to her.'

'Wasn't it see-through and tickly and sticky? It sounds horrible!'

'Can't have been. Not for Queen Victoria.'

'Did she ever wear it?'

'I don't know. She might have liked it better if they'd made a dress woven out of spider silk. You can get spider silk from their cocoons, like with silkworms, only spider silk is better. It's finer and it's stronger. They're trying to use it to make bullet-proof vests.'

'If spider silk's so good, why don't you see things made out of it in the shops?'

'Because it takes nearly twenty-eight thousand spiders to make just half a kilo of silk, that's why. Then you've got to feed them all on loads of flies . . .'

'Yuk!'

' . . . and the biggest problem is that you'd have to keep them all separate or they'd eat each other!'

'Oh, no. Not bloomin' eating spiders again! Are you making it up?'

'No, it's true.'

Izzy looked doubtful.

'Want to bet on it?' offered Andrew.

'No I do not! Come on, let's post my thing.'

Izzy took the pink envelope out of her bag and pushed it through the letterbox in Underwear World's door. It landed on the other side with a small dull plop.

'Right. Back to the bus stop,' said Andrew, but Izzy wasn't ready to go. That small plop didn't feel right. It wasn't the important sort of sound it should be for claiming a bagful of real jewels and entering a big money prize draw. Izzy hesitated. She didn't want to leave things there; to come away with empty hands and return to school where Andrew would pal up with Sam again. She was enjoying herself and, besides, she'd just had a brilliant idea.

'Why don't we get the jewels now, while we're here? Then I'll be able to give them to Mum tomorrow.'

'No.'

Andrew started walking back up Union Lane, but Izzy was already pushing the bell beside the big wooden door. There was a buzz and a deep voice from nowhere said, 'Yes?'

'Oh,' said Izzy, 'er, I've come to fetch something.'

Andrew was beckoning from up the road. 'Come *on*, Izz. You promised.'

'What name?' asked the voice.

Izzy put her mouth near to the metal slits. 'Izzy,' she said. 'Isobel Bonnet, *Ms* Isobel Bonnet.'

'Izz!' Andrew was beside her now.

'Who do you wish to see, Ms Bonnet?'

I'm not wishing now, thought Izzy. I'm doing. 'Mr Tom Bottomly, please. He wrote to me.'

'Izz! Come on!'

'I see. Come in and I will contact Mr Bottomly for you.'

Buzzz, click, the big door opened a small way and Izzy took a step forward. Andrew held her from behind.

'Don't be stupid, Izz. We've got to get back or we'll be in real trouble.'

Izzy shook off Andrew's hand and whispered back, 'Look, you're not the leader now. You stay here if you like, but I'm going in for the jewels.' She pushed on through the door and Andrew followed her.

A man in uniform sat behind a desk. A sign, which said RECEPTION, hung above him. He had a little label on his broad blue chest that said CARL. Carl was tall and thin and strong and had orange hair. He rolled his eyes upwards when he saw Izzy and Andrew.

'You are Ms Bonnet?' he asked.

'That's me,' said Izzy. 'I've come to collect the jewels that Mr Bottomly has for me.'

'Oh yes?'

'It said in the letter that he would send the

jewels, but since I am here I thought I would save him the postage and take them today. I'm going to give them to my mother for her birthday.'

'Really,' said Carl, getting up from behind his desk. He towered over Izzy. Izzy took a step back so that she could still look him in the face.

'Yes, really,' she said. 'Look!' She waved the bumph letter at him. Carl took it and looked at it briefly.

'I see,' he said. 'And how old are you, young lady?'

Andrew was shuffling behind Izzy.

'We ought to be going, Izz,' he said in a tight sort of voice, but Izzy was getting cross.

'Can I speak to Mr Bottomly, please?'

'Shouldn't you be at school? Does your mother know that you're here?' Carl knotted his arms over his chest and glared down at her.

'My mother is outside, waiting in the car and school have let me have the morning off. Now, please can I see Mr Bottomly?' Behind her, Andrew made an odd noise that he turned into a cough. Carl's gaze slid slowly from Izzy's face to Andrew's.

'And you, son. Who are you?'

Andrew gawped like a fish. He's frightened, Izzy realised. Well, I'm not! I'm not going to be bullied by Carl just because he's big. It's none of his business who we are!

'He's my friend,' she said, before Andrew could answer for himself. 'He's called Sam. He's at the same school as me.'

'And which school is that?'

'It's – it's – Queen Victoria Primary School,' said Izzy. 'And my teacher is Mrs Flint. She's got ginger hair and she's very kind and . . .'

'And where is this Queen Victoria school?'

'Over that way,' said Izzy, pointing vaguely out of the building.

The arm was caught by Andrew who tried to drag her towards the door.

'We can't wait any longer, I'm afraid. Must go.' he said.

A door opened behind them.

'Is this the young lady, Carl?' asked a new voice, and Izzy turned to see a very round man.

He reminded Izzy of those toy clowns that you try to push over and they always bob upright again, but this man wore a businessman's double-breasted suit of grey stripy material. He had the sharp eye of a businessman under what Mum would call a pudding-basin haircut. The hair hung limply the same length all around his fat head like a lampshade fringe. It was a little boy's haircut and looked very strange with the suit and the canny eyes.

Carl pointed to Izzy.

'This, sir, is the very young lady and this,' he pointed to Andrew, 'is apparently her friend Stan.'

'Sam,' said Izzy.

The round man looked at his watch, then turned to Izzy and Andrew.

'Good, good,' he said. 'And I'm Tom Bottomly, manager of Underwear World. Come to my office, both of you. I can give you five minutes for your project or whatever it is. Come along.'

'Thank you,' said Izzy, and she shot a look of triumph up at Carl. Carl's green eyes looked steadily back without blinking.

'And I'll just pop outside and tell Ms Bonnet's mother that she won't be long,' he said.

Set up one lie and you must add more lies to prop it up. Lie Spider smiled with delight as Izzy's lies multiplied. Round and round he spun until his web was complete; his trap set.

7 Into the web

Izzy followed Mr Bottomly's fat bottom. He waddled like a duck in a suit. Izzy was enjoying herself now, but Andrew was twitching behind her.

'We've got to be quick, Izz!'

Mr Bottomly pushed through a door and held it open to invite Izzy and Andrew in. With its flowery sofa and sunset views on the wall, the office looked more like Nan's front room than a real office. There was a tray on the desk. It was neatly laid with a teapot, milk jug, sugar bowl and a fine, thin cup and saucer. There was even a paper doily on a plate with two Jammy Dodgers on it.

'Would you like a biscuit?' asked Mr Bottomly. 'Or a drink? I've got some fizzy pop somewhere.'

Izzy was tempted, but she could feel Andrew, tight with worry beside her.

'No thank you very much,' said Izzy. 'I've just come to collect the bag of jewels.'

'To collect jewels, eh?' said Mr Bottomly. Then, as he eased himself on to the desk chair, his fat face wobbled a laugh. 'Would that be the jewels from our autumn promotion?'

Izzy didn't see why that should be funny. 'Yes,' she said. 'The bumph says that there's a bag of jewels with my name on it. Please could I take it now?'

'No, my dear, you can't! Those jewels are for my special customers who have completed and returned the claim form,' said Mr Bottomly.

'I have,' said Izzy. 'I posted the Yes, Please! envelope just now.'

'But the offer was only sent to grown-ups, my dear, not to little girls. Now, I suggest that you and your friend here each take one of these biscuits and go back to wherever you should be.'

'Thank you,' said Andrew. 'We'd better be going.' He headed for the door.

'No! Wait!' said Izzy. 'I am not a little girl and I don't want biscuits. I'm a person and I want jewels! Your offer was sent to Ms Isobel Bonnet at 5 Daisy Road. *I* am Ms Isobel Bonnet and *I* live at 5 Daisy Road! So you have to give them to me, don't you?'

Mr Bottomly took a large silk handkerchief from his pocket and wiped under his floppy fringe. His small eyes flicked between Izzy and Andrew. He opened his mouth to say something but was stopped by a knock at the door and Carl's deep voice asking, 'Could I have a quick word please, sir?'

Mr Bottomly got up and went out into the corridor to speak to Carl.

'Izz!' hissed Andrew. 'We've got to get out!'

'Why?'

Izzy had just noticed a box behind Mr Bottomly's desk. It had *Autumn Promotion* written on it in big marker-pen letters and, under that and in smaller letters, *gemstone waste*.

'Because that Carl man knows that you were

lying!' said Andrew. 'Because we should be at school. Because Mr What's-his-name isn't even going to give you any jewels. He was embarassed. I don't believe there even are any jewels.'

Izzy looked at the box. Cardboard flaps hid whatever was inside it. She looked towards the door. She could just see a slice of the two men talking in the gap between the door edge and the wall. With one eye on the men and her tongue between her teeth, Izzy took one tiptoe step to reach the box. She bent down and silently lifted a flap.

'What on earth are you doing now?' squeaked Andrew.

In the box were hundreds of little bags.

'It's the jewels!' whispered Izzy triumphantly. 'See!'

The tiny, maroon velvet bags had golden drawstrings pinching them closed at the top. They looked like fairies' shoe bags. Each one had a white tag hanging from the drawstring, but the tags were blank. There were no names on any of them and they were surprisingly small and limp. The bumph picture had made them look fatter and bigger. Perhaps the jewels hadn't been put in them yet? Izzy reached down and took a bag. She was about to pull the neck of the bag open when she heard her name being spoken out in the corridor.

' . . . Isobel something,' said the deep voice of Carl. Izzy froze and listened as he continued: 'Yes, here on the letter – Isobel Bonnet.'

There was a grumble of words from Mr Bottomly that Izzy couldn't make out, then Carl's clearer voice again.

' "Friend," she said.' Carl laughed. 'I wouldn't believe it, sir. Looked like a brother to me – like two peas in a pod, those two, sir. And there's no such school as Queen Victoria Primary School in the phone book. Do you want me to call the police?'

Police! Izzy looked at Andrew. His face looked like she felt – as if somebody had pulled out her plug and all her insides had drained away. They must hide or get away fast. But how?

Andrew grabbed Izzy's sleeve, and pulled her behind Mr Bottomly's flowery sofa. They crouched there, trying not to breathe as the door opened again.

'Hey!' said Mr Bottomly. 'Where have you kids got to? Isobel? Sam?'

Mr Bottomly can't have any children of his own, thought Izzy. Behind the sofa was such an obvious place to hide.

Mr Bottomly slammed around, checking the window and behind the door, then he shouted for Carl and Izzy closed her eyes tight. Carl would know. Carl would take two steps into the room, grab them by the neck, and pull them out from behind the sofa. But Carl didn't reply straight away.

'Carl?' shouted Mr Bottomly again, and he went through the door to search for him.

Immediately, Andrew was up and making for the door, dragging Izzy after him. He peered cautiously round the door, then swung it open. They dodged down the corridor in the opposite direction from Mr Bottomly, heading deeper into the building. As they ran past two glass doors Izzy glimpsed great banks of machines rumbling and pounding with people working at them. She would have liked to see what they were doing, but Andrew was hauling her away and up some stairs. There was an EXIT sign on the wall with a picture of a man running and an arrow pointing downstairs. That's where Izzy wanted to go, but Andrew was pulling her upwards.

There was a shout from downstairs and the stamp of running feet. Carl was after them! Izzy shot up the last three steps like a firework rocket.

'Come on!' hissed Andrew, his voice hidden by the noise of machines. But there was suddenly nowhere to go. At the top of the stairs was a glass door. Izzy could see rows of women sitting at sewing-machines. There would be no escape past them. There was another door but that one had NO ADMITTANCE written on it and a big padlock hung beside its handle.

Carl's voice boomed down below and Izzy grabbed the handle anyway, twisted it hard and pushed. Magically, the door opened. The padlock had been hanging loose, not actually holding anything together. Quick as kittens after kippers, Izzy and Andrew slipped past the door, then turned together to push it firmly shut. Then they leaned against it, ears listening hard. Izzy braced herself ready to hold the door closed if Carl tried pushing from the other side. She held her breath as his heavy footsteps paused on the other side of the door and then there was a squeak and a thud as he pushed through the door to the sewing-room. All there was to be heard now was the clatter of the factory dimmed to a hum by the thick door.

Carl had gone, at least for the moment. Izzy let out her breath and felt Andrew, beside her, do the same. In front of her was a thick, musty darkness. There might be a room in front of them or a wall, or there might even be a big hole. You couldn't tell. Izzy wanted to test the space with a sound, but she stayed quiet, only gradually relaxing as time passed and nobody came pushing at the other side of the door. After a while she felt safe enough to whisper, 'What do we do now?'

'Go on up, I suppose.'

Izzy looked and found that her eyes had adjusted a little to the dark. She could just make out steps rising up in front of her. She reached forward for the stair rail and began to climb up the dusty dark space.

'Why do you think this is all shut off?' she asked Andrew in a whisper.

'Don't know. Perhaps they just don't need the room. Or it might be fire regulations or something.'

'Does that mean there isn't any way out?'

'Might do.'

At the top of the stairs Izzy pushed open another door and they stepped into a vast hall of a room. Their steps echoed and Andrew raised a finger to his lips. The wooden floor was stained and holed in a regular pattern where machines had once been bolted to the floor. Now there was nothing, but the noise from downstairs seemed to Izzy to be the ghostly thinned noise of machines from long ago.

Andrew turned to Izzy. 'We're trapped, Izz. Completely trapped.'

The web had done its job. They were caught. Watch for a while, thought Lie Spider. Then go in for the kill.

8 Trapped!

They searched the empty factory floor. Its dimness and mustiness and the echoey height of its ceiling made Izzy feel as if she were in a church. She could only whisper in this place. There were rows of windows on each side of the room, each made up of small panes covered in years of grime and dust. Sunlight came and went, beaming checkered patches of light on to the floor and then snatching them away again. Izzy longed to look out, but the windows were too high. In the far corner of the room was a boarded-up door and beside it were a rickety old kitchen chair, an empty coca cola can and a crisp packet. Izzy imagined the workman who had boarded the door having his lunch on that chair.

Izzy wanted to find solid relics of days gone by. All she found were the ghosts of past workers who seemed to live in the movement of light and air. Small breezes stroked over her skin when she walked in parts of the room. Izzy didn't ask Andrew if he could feel them too.

Andrew had dumped his schoolbag by the rickety chair and was balanced on the edge of it, elbows on knees and chin on cupped hands.

'Don't worry,' said Izzy. 'We'll get out.'

'How?'

'We can get out when they go off for lunch, can't we?'

Andrew looked completely miserable as he replied quietly, 'I don't think places like this close for lunch. We're completely and totally and absolutely stuck.'

'I suppose you think its all my fault, don't you?' said Izzy. She wished he would shout at her, be her bossy big brother, call her stupid and tell her what they should do.

'Well, it is your fault.' Andrew still didn't raise his voice.

'I suppose you want me to say sorry.'

'I don't see how that would help.'

'Look, if they don't go off at lunch-time then we can get out when they leave work.'

'Izzy, they'll lock the place up and put on burglar alarms. And, anyway, that won't be for hours. Mum will be expecting us home from school before then. We'll just have to give ourselves up.'

'No!' Izzy thought of Carl the giant, of the police, of Mum, of school, of the toe-curling embarrassment. 'No, please. Let's not.' Izzy looked at her watch. 'Look, it's half past eleven now, so let's at least wait for lunch-time and see what happens. Please, Andrew!'

He thought for a moment. 'All right, we'll wait for two hours. Two boring hours, and then we go and give ourselves up.'

'Thanks!' Izzy sat down, cross-legged, on the dusty floor, back against the wall. Safe for the moment and two hours to think up a way to escape. She could enjoy the adventure of it again. She just wished that Andrew would share that feeling, but he still looked glum. 'I'll tell you a really good joke,' she said.

'Go on then.'

'What's invisible and smells of bananas?'

'Don't know.'

'A monkey's burp!'

Andrew's mouth twitched into an almost-smile, so Izzy carried on.

'What's yellow and stupid?'

'You in that jumper!'

'No! Thick custard! Your turn.'

'OK. What do you get when you cross a sheep with a kangaroo?'

'Everyone knows that one! It's a woolly jumper.'

'Yep. Do you know any more?'

'No.'

'Nor do I.'

For a while they sat in silence. Specks of dust glinted and swam in the sunlight. Izzy remembered Mum once saying how she and Dad always seemed to make their big decisions when they were driving somewhere. It was because they sat close together in a car, but didn't look at each other, and were strapped down. You couldn't go off and do something else in the middle of a conversation. Just like me and Andrew now, thought Izzy. So Izzy decided to ask Andrew an important question.

'What do you want to do when you grow up?'

Andrew looked surprised, but he thought for a moment.

'Something different from Mum and Dad,' he said. 'I don't want to work in an office. I'd like to be a scientist and discover something that nobody's ever found before. Perhaps something to do with spiders.' He looked warily at Izzy, but Izzy didn't laugh.

'You'll do it! You know so much about them already.'

'But there's loads more to learn.' Andrew hugged his knees to his chest and rested his head sideways on them to face Izzy. 'Do you know, there are about thirty-five thousand different kinds of spider that have been discovered? The experts reckon that there are at least that many more still to find!'

'You might have to explore jungles to find them!'

'I know. It'd be great.'

'I'll miss you when you go.'

'No, you won't. You'll be grown up yourself by then. We won't even be living in the same house as each other, so it won't make much difference if I'm in the same country or not. Anyway, what do you want to do?'

Izzy thought for a moment. Having a job was too far away to think about now. Her dreams were all more immediate. 'I want to go back to sharing a room with you instead of Grace.'

Andrew laughed. 'Do you still want that?'

'Yes. It's not fair that Mum and Dad made me share with the baby!' Izzy could feel the old fury rising up inside her again.

'It wasn't their fault,' said Andrew. 'It was me. I didn't want to share with you, and I still don't!'

'*You*? Why? I thought . . .'

'Because my room is the only place where I can get away from you. You pester me all the time, Izz. At home, at school, you're always there, butting in when I'm with my friends or wanting me to do one of your stupid games when I'm trying to read or . . .' Then Andrew saw Izzy's face. She looked as if he had hit her. 'Sorry, Izz, but you do.' And the worst thing was that Izzy suddenly realised it was true. She did pester Andrew, just as Grace pestered her.

'Why didn't you tell me before?'

'I did. I'm always telling you not to be a pest.'

'But I didn't know you meant it!'

Andrew shrugged. Then Izzy took a deep breath. 'It doesn't matter any more. Grace isn't so bad now she's getting bigger. And, anyway, my dream is to get enough money to buy a big house with rooms for everyone so I don't have to share at all. I want a space that is just mine.'

'How are you going to do that? You're not going to get any prize money now, are you?'

'I know. I'll do it some other way. I think I'll make one of those Christmas books that sells millions and millions of copies. It'll be called *A Book Of Dreams* and I'll write to all sorts of famous people and get them to tell me what their biggest dream is.'

'I can never remember my dreams when I wake up.'

'No, not that kind of dream. I mean hopes-and-wishes sort of dreams. Like you wanting to discover spiders.'

'And whose dreams will you collect?'

'I'd like to know what the Queen dreams of. I expect she'd like to run off into the mountains and live in a cave with nobody fussing around her.'

'Who else?'

Izzy rested her chin on the heels of her hands. 'The people whose dreams I'd really like to know about aren't the famous ones, but I'd need famous ones for a book.'

'Who do you really want to know about?' asked Andrew.

'You. And the teachers at school, and Mum and Dad. Do you think Dad dreams of being a painter instead of an engineer? I do. And I bet Mum dreams of looking really beautiful so that everybody turns to look. That's why I wanted that bag of jewels.'

'I don't think she cares much about jewels. She never wears any.'

'That's because she hasn't got any!'

'She hasn't got any because she'd rather get other things.'

Had Mum *chosen* not to sparkle? 'We'll ask her when we get home.' said Izzy. 'Home.' Izzy jumped up. 'I'm going to open this door.'

The boarded-up door was just beside them and tempting draughts of fresh air and freedom blew from between the boarding and the wall. Izzy reached up and pulled at the chipboard. It didn't move.

'You need a lever.' Andrew got up and rummaged in his schoolbag. 'Shove this under the gap, then pull.' He handed Izzy his ruler. She tried it. It snapped as soon as she pulled with any strength.

'Ow!' she said, sucking at her fingers. 'It isn't going to move.'

'Yes, it will,' said Andrew, getting up and taking a look. 'There's only thin nails holding it. We just need a stronger lever. There must be something we could use.'

Izzy pounced. 'Here!' She wrenched a loose strut from between the legs of the rickety chair. 'Would this do?'

Andrew took the strut, reached up, and pushed one end of it into the gap between the door and the chipboard. Then he pulled. Nothing happened. He counted to three and pulled again, going red in the face with effort, and at last something shifted.

'It's coming!'

But it only moved a little way.

'It's not going to work,' said Izzy.

'Yes it is, stupid! We've just got to try, try again 'til it comes all the way out.'

'Got to what?'

'You know, Robert the Bruce!'

Izzy looked blank, so Andrew explained.

'Robert the Bruce was King of Scotland, stupid! A spider tried again and again to spin a thread across a gap and in the end she did it. That gave Robert the Bruce the idea to try again to beat the English army.'

'And did it work?'

'Yep. He beat the English at the Battle of Bannockburn.'

'Why did you say "she" for the spider?'

'Because female spiders are bigger and

stronger than male ones. They make the best webs.'

'Then I'm probably stronger than you! Come on, let me do it too.'

They stood together and pulled and heaved on the chair strut, first in one top corner of the chipboard, then in the other and at last the board groaned and moved, flapping away from the top of the door. Izzy rested her head against the wall and peered round the board to see the tatty remains of a door. It had warped and didn't quite fit its doorway any more. Air and light from outside came in around the edges and the word EXIT was peeling off.

'Come on!' said Andrew. 'If we just pull the board downwards, the bottom nails will come out. You stand on the chair and do it and I'll catch the board when it falls so that it doesn't crash down.'

Izzy climbed on to the rickety chair and took hold of the board. Andrew put his palms against the board and braced his legs.

'Are you all right on that thing?' he asked.

'I think so,' answered Izzy, but the chair

wibbled and wobbled every time she moved. 'At least it's not far to fall!'

'I'm not worried about you getting hurt! I'm worried that you'll land with a bloomin' great crash and give away where we are.'

'Oh, thank you very much.'

Izzy heaved at the heavy chipboard and it suddenly came away from the wall. It fell, pushing Izzy so that Izzy, the board and the chair all fell together on to Andrew, who tried to catch them all. As she fell, Izzy saw the board bounce off the top of Andrew's head. Down came Andrew, the board and Izzy in a nightmare slow-motion ballet, landing in a heap on the dusty floor.

For a moment or two Izzy lay gasping for breath. I must get up, she thought. She stirred stiffly, hurting on knees and elbows. Her shaky hands found it hard to push the heavy board off her.

'At least you gave it a soft landing!' Izzy told Andrew in a wavery voice. 'Do you think they heard?'

There was no answer.

'Andrew?'

Andrew wasn't moving. His eyes were closed. He looked like a doll, shiny white in the light that beamed through the dusty windows. Izzy crouched down and stroked the back of a finger down his cheek.

'Andrew?'

His skin was cold and clammy as a rubber glove. He was very, very still. But something did move. A bright red finger of blood trickled steadily through the jungle of hair on his head. Izzy watched it – up and over, in and out the red wove through the hairs and on down until it dripped on to the dusty floorboards.

'Andrew!' Izzy shook him. 'Andrew, if you die, I'll kill you!'

He didn't move.

Lie Spider darted into the centre of the web, in and out, just pausing long enough to bite and poison. Then he retreated to watch and wait. So long as nothing interfered, the poison would dissolve his prey from the inside and Lie Spider

would suck them hollow. He licked his lips and
waited.

9 Breaking the threads

Izzy had never felt so alone in her whole life. Her hands clutched each other for comfort. 'Andrew, wake up, you stupid . . .!' She put one hand over her mouth and tried to hold in a sob that was breaking out. She was doing this all wrong! She wanted to run away, wanted to undo the accident. But the accident had happened and she was trapped with it.

Do something, she told herself. Look and see what needs to be done, and do it. She looked. The blood glistened as it moved. Izzy took off her coat and laid it over Andrew, but not over his head. She tucked the coat firmly under his chin. Andrew still didn't move. 'Oh, please!'

She *needed* him, didn't he know that? 'You've got to wake up, you stupid . . .!'

Andrew moved. He stirred and moaned. His eyes flickered open, shut, open and then found Izzy. His eyes reminded Izzy of the eyes of a rabbit they had hit with the car one night. Dad had got out of the car and picked up the rabbit and it hadn't struggled at all. It had just looked at them with pleading eyes and then it had died in Dad's hands.

'You're all right!' Izzy told him. 'Aren't you?'

Andrew didn't say anything. He slowly lifted one arm from under Izzy's coat and put his hand up to his head. Then he brought the hand in front of his face and he looked at it. It was scarlet with bright blood. He looked at Izzy with those eyes again.

'Shall I bandage it?' she asked brightly. 'Yes, a bandage would be a good idea. It'll stop the bleeding,' she answered herself. But where could she find a bandage? They would have them downstairs in the factory, of course, but that would mean trouble with Carl and probably the police and certainly Mum and Dad. No, she would sort it out by herself up here. Izzy patted her pockets, hoping to feel a hankie in one. There was something. It was soft, but it scrunched grittily between her fingers. Izzy pulled the thing out and stared at what lay in her hand. The tiny velvet bag from Mr Bottomly's office! The scrunch inside it must be the jewels!

'I'm a jewel thief,' whispered Izzy. 'I've stolen jewels.'

Andrew's hand pulled at her ankle. 'Please, Izz...' He was beginning to shake.

'I'm looking for a bandage,' said Izzy. 'I'll soon have you bandaged up and then you'll feel better.'

She pushed the jewel bag back into her pocket and looked around for her schoolbag. It wasn't there. Of course – it was in Mr Bottomly's office! Izzy closed her eyes and saw in her mind the label inside her bag shouting her name, address, telephone number and school in her neatest, clearest handwriting. Mr Bottomly must know everything. He must have telephoned home and school and . . .

'Izz!'

Andrew mustn't know how stupid she'd been. A bandage. Izzy bit on her lip and grabbed Andrew's schoolbag and tipped it upside down. Out came a shower of books and pens and sweet papers and a jumbly pile of football kit. Izzy plonked the T-shirt on to the place on Andrew's head where blood still bubbled out. 'Hold that,' she said, trying to keep her voice from shaking. Andrew's hand, sticky with blood, obediently held the pad in place.

'Izz!'

Izzy took the two thick football socks and knotted them together. She placed the knot on top of the pad and brought the socks down round Andrew's face and knotted them under his chin.

'Like Nan's rain hat!' she said brightly.

'Feel sick,' mumbled Andrew. He was hitching himself up on to elbows and leaning over to one side. He gasped deep, quivering breaths.

'Here!' said Izzy. She took hold of Andrew's lunch box, took off the lid, tipped everything out of it and offered the box to Andrew as a sick bowl. He was sick. The smell made Izzy feel sick too. She held her breath and put the lid back on the box.

'Better out than in!' said Izzy. 'You'll feel much better after that!'

Andrew didn't reply. He slumped back down to the floor. He shook all over. There was blood seeping through the bandage.

'D'you want something to eat?' asked Izzy. He must replace all that blood, she thought.

'No,' said Andrew. It seemed to take a lot of effort for him to speak. 'Izz . . .'

'A drink?' she offered. 'It's clean inside the bottle.'

'Izz!'

'Yes?'

'Get help.'

'We don't need help! We're managing fine on our own!' Izzy's heart was beating extra fast.

'Tell them! Tell them downstairs.'

'Let's just wait a bit. You'll feel better soon.' Andrew didn't know that she was a jewel thief. He didn't know that Mr Bottomly and Carl knew who she was and that there were probably policemen searching for her by now.

'I feel funny,' said Andrew.

'You look . . .' but Izzy didn't finish what she was going to say because she had let herself look into Andrew's eyes. They didn't look at her. They moved, but not together. Andrew wasn't in them any more. Izzy jumped up. 'I'll get help,' she said.

She could see a metal platform and railing through a hole in the newly revealed EXIT door. A rusty metal ladder zigzagged down from it. Perhaps she could escape down the ladder now? Down the metal steps, then run to the nearest phone box to dial 999? But the broken door wouldn't open when Izzy tugged at it. Perhaps she should go down inside the building after all, slide quickly and silently down the banisters before Carl had time to get up from his desk, then run . . . But, no! You're being stupid again, Izz! Stupid, stupid! Stop it! Stop everything spiralling bigger and spinning out of control!

'Izz . . .' moaned Andrew.

'I'm going! I'm going to tell them everything!'

Izzy ran across the room, down the stairs and

pushed out through the NO ADMITTANCE door into the noise of the factory. She stumbled down the stairs, and ran to Mr Bottomly's office. She pushed the door open without knocking. Mr Bottomly was at his desk, a pen in one hand, a Jammy Dodger in the other.

'You're still here!' he said.

Izzy glanced behind Mr Bottomly. There was her schoolbag, untouched where she had left it behind his sofa. So he didn't know after all. He didn't know who they were or what they'd done or . . . But that didn't make any difference. Only the truth could rescue Andrew!

Mr Bottomly gawped at her.

'Please,' said Izzy. 'I've got to get help! I've done it all wrong! We went through this door that said NO ADMITTANCE on it and I don't think we're really allowed through there . . .'

'No, you are not!' said Mr Bottomly, but Izzy carried on.

' . . . We went there because Carl was chasing us. And I've stolen your jewels by accident and – please . . .' Izzy gasped for breath, '. . . oh, please get an ambulance, because Andrew's hurt! There's blood and his eyes have gone funny!'

'Who on earth is Andrew?'

'He's my brother, not a friend called Sam. Oh, please help him! None of it's his fault!'

Mr Bottomly put down his biscuit and stood up.

'Carl!' shouted Mr Bottomly.

'Yes, sir?' Carl appeared in the doorway.

'The girl tells me that the boy is up on the top storey and he's been hurt. Have a look at him, will you, and get him downstairs.'

'He shouldn't be moved! He needs an ambulance!' said Izzy.

Mr Bottomly looked at her hard from under his fringe.

'I'll call an ambulance,' he said. 'But I want the boy downstairs when they arrive.'

'Understood, sir,' said Carl, and he headed for the stairs.

'I'll help,' said Izzy, but Mr Bottomly held up a hand.

'Not so fast, young lady! I want your parents' telephone number. The *real* number.'

Izzy couldn't bear the thought of Mum being frightened by a phone call telling her that Andrew was badly hurt. It would have to be Dad. She gave Dad's work telephone number, then ran after Carl.

Lie Spider watched in amazement. As truth after truth was told, the fine threads of his web broke, releasing his prey and dropping it into the unknown. If his victims fell on to hard ground, then Lie Spider would still get his meal. If not, he would go hungry.

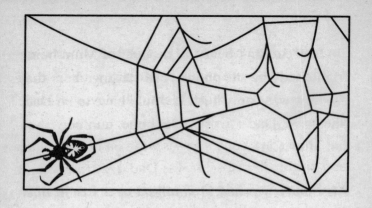

10 Bigger flies to trap

'I don't think we should be moving him!' Izzy told Carl, but he ignored her. He picked Andrew up with easy strength and carried him down the stairs as if he were a large floppy doll. Izzy held the doors open and hurried along behind. Andrew was laid down on Mr Bottomly's sofa. Izzy knelt beside him.

'It's all right now,' she told him. 'They know everything. An ambulance is coming.' The ambulance people arrived, pushing Izzy to one side and screening Andrew from her with their backs. They put a mask over his mouth and loaded him on to a stretcher. It's my fault he's been hurt, thought Izzy. She looked out of the window, up at the clouds, and made a bargain with God. If you let Andrew be all right, I'll never ever lie again.

Then somebody's hands were on her shoulder and pulling her close. It was Dad. Izzy turned and held on tight while Dad talked over her head to Mr Bottomly, Carl and the ambulance people. Dad led Izzy out to the car and strapped her into the seat as he had used to do when she was very young. Then his big hands took gentle hold of each side of her head.

'Tell me, Izzy,' he said. 'Are you OK?'

She nodded.

'Good,' he said and shut her door. Neither of them said any more as they followed the ambulance. They parked the car and, holding hands, followed Andrew's stretcher into the hospital. Andrew was taken into a small cubicle and a nurse asked Izzy and Dad to wait outside.

'We'll just stitch him up. The doctor will look at him and then you can go in. Don't worry,' she said. 'He'll be right as rain in no time!'

'I'd better telephone Mum,' said Dad.

Izzy watched Dad on the telephone, telling, soothing. Why hadn't she been able to talk to Andrew like that? To be gentle and honest? Izzy knotted herself with crossed arms and legs.

'Mum's on her way,' said Dad. He sat down and took a deep breath.

'Now then, Izz. I want you to take those things out of your hair so that you look like my Izzy again, and then I want you to tell me exactly what happened. Mr Bottomly told me that he came to the rescue when Andrew was hurt. He called the ambulance, didn't he? But what in the world happened before that?' Dad held out his hands as if he was begging. 'What on earth were the two of you doing, Izz? Why weren't you at school? And how did Andrew get hurt?'

Izzy pulled the hairband and elastic ties from her hair and shook it loose. The floppy fringe gave her a place to hide from Dad's piercing look, but Izzy didn't want to hide. She wanted to make Dad understand, so she pushed the hair aside and told him everything, slowly and clearly. She told him how she had lied about Mum's present. She told him about the bumph in the dustbin and she showed him the crumpled glossy promises that she still had in her backpack. Dad looked at them and shook his head. She told him about Mr Bottomly and Carl and about going through the door that should have been locked. Then she told him about the accident. As she talked, Dad put a hand up to his head, as if feeling Andrew's injury on himself, but he didn't say anything. He didn't interrupt, so Izzy carried on and told him everything. She told him how she had done everything wrong when Andrew was hurt. She even told him about the jewels.

'Look,' she said, and she put a hand in her pocket and pulled out the tiny velvet bag with the scrunchy jewels inside. 'I've stolen these by mistake. I didn't mean to take them.'

Dad spoke at last, but quietly.

'Good Lord, Izz! Truancy, trespassing, vandalism, and now stealing!' He sat back in his seat, shaking his head and snorting a disbelieving laugh. He took the tiny velvet bag from Izzy and weighed its slight weight up and down in one hand. 'I can't quite believe all this!' he said. 'In fact I don't believe it! Why on earth would anybody give away jewels? Have you looked inside this bag?'

Izzy shook her head.

'Come on, then.' Dad pulled the neck of the tiny bag open with his big fingers.

'No!' said Izzy. She could feel the tangle of trouble closing in. It had caught Andrew. She didn't want it to trap Dad too. He mustn't handle stolen goods!

But Dad was already tipping the little bag upside down over the low table in front of them. A stream of tiny gritty bits poured itself into a minute pyramid. Izzy gasped, 'Sand!'

Dad pushed the pyramid with a finger and put his head down and to one side to look at the grains more closely.

'Not sand,' he said. 'I can see different colours.' Then he laughed. 'You know what these are? These are your genuine diamonds, sapphires and rubies, Izz!'

'But they're tiny! They were much bigger in the picture!'

'I bet they were! But there's nothing in the writing about size, is there? It only states that you will get genuine gems. And you have. You've got completely worthless, but genuine jewels. I bet these are the bits they trim off when they cut bigger jewels into shape. Just sweepings off the floor.'

'Oh,' said Izzy. Dad laughed.

'Cheer up! At least that Bottomly fellow isn't going to chase after you for these!' He poked at the gem dust and laughed again and this time the laugh caught the tiny gems in its wind and gusted them off the tabletop and away.

'Dad!'

They had gone. The diamonds, rubies and sapphires were lost in the everyday dust on the floor. Dust to dust. Those grains of rubbish were what she had risked Andrew's life for! Izzy tried to smile with Dad's laugh, but her smile wobbled. She leaned her head on Dad's shoulder and let hot tears wash through her muddle of feelings. I'm sorry, Andrew, she thought. I'm sorry, sorry, sorry. She didn't know whether Andrew could read her thoughts as he lay on the other side of the cubicle wall. In the old days she would have known, but that link had gone, and Izzy cried for that too. She cried for what she had lost and for what she had done. She had hurt Andrew and Dad today in different ways. Izzy suddenly wanted Grace, straightforward, simple, honest Grace. Grace wouldn't mind what Izzy had done today. She wouldn't need explanations or apologies. But Mum would. Izzy looked up from Dad's shoulder.

'What will Mum say?'

Dad looked down and smiled. 'I think you know exactly what Mum will say.'

'She'll say, "It's lucky I love you!" '

That was what Mum always said when any of them did anything bad, but by mistake.

'But, Izzy!' Dad's voice was stern. 'Before Mum gets here, I want to know why you did it. I don't understand why you deceived us and skipped school, even if you did think that the jewels were proper ones.'

'It was for the money as well! I wanted to buy us a better house.'

'A better house?' Dad laughed an unfunny laugh. 'Don't you like home?'

Izzy thought of home. She could picture in

her mind every bit of the house, every smell, every crack and every creaking stair.

'I love it,' she said.

'Then why . . .?'

'I just wanted somewhere with enough bedrooms for us to have one each!'

'Oh, Izz. Still that?' Dad pushed a hand through his hair. 'I didn't realise that this bedroom business was so important to you.' He thought for a moment. 'If it makes you so very unhappy to share with Grace, then perhaps I should throw away all my old painting stuff and move my work into a corner of our bedroom. Then we could turn the study into a little bedroom for you.'

'No!' The whole fuss seemed silly now. 'I like Grace sometimes. It's only difficult when I'm trying to do something important and she spoils it.'

'Then how about me giving you time in the study to do your important things? Would that solve it? Perhaps a couple of hours each weekend?'

'That would be nice.'

'And, Izzy.' Dad was holding up a finger.

'Yes?'

'Don't ever, ever, ever go off alone like that again! Understand?'

'I won't.'

'Good.' Then Dad looked towards the door. 'Look who's here!'

Mum, pale and hurrying, came through the door with Grace dragging at one hand. Izzy ran and hugged them both.

'How's Andrew?' asked Mum. 'What happened? Oh, Izzy.' Mum ruffled Izzy's hair. 'What a girl you are! It's lucky that I love you, isn't it!'

Lie Spider's prey had landed softly, caught in a net of another kind; a web of love. But Lie Spider didn't mind. He had a particularly large and juicy new fly in his sights; a fly who was an expert at lying. He hid his lies in truths. Lie Spider liked that. 'Treasure the Truth' was his motto. Keep the truth safely locked away where nobody will find it. Lie Spider rubbed his eight hands together and polished his fangs. The girl's family were welcome to have her back. There were bigger flies to trap.

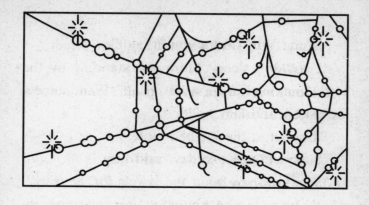

11 Jewelled threads

Andrew was home, laughing and teasing, but pale. That night in bed Izzy's mind fizzed with thoughts about the accident. She remembered over and over again how the blood had bubbled from Andrew's head. She thought of the things she should have done, the things she should have said to him. Then she thought about Mum and how she hadn't got anything to give her now. Izzy tossed and turned for hours with those thoughts until she finally gave up trying to sleep. It was very early, but she couldn't lie in bed any longer. She tiptoed down the stairs and into the kitchen.

'Hello, love. Happy birthday!'

'Mum! Why aren't you in bed?'

'I couldn't sleep.' Mum was standing by the kettle, making herself a hot drink. 'Want some?' she asked, and Izzy nodded.

They sat at the kitchen table.

'Sorry about yesterday,' said Izzy.

'What did you want the jewels for, anyway?' asked Mum. 'You're a bit young for wearing posh jewellery.'

'It wasn't for me. It was for you.'

'Me! Why?'

'For your birthday. It was to make up for your funny engagement ring.'

'But I love my ring!' said Mum, and she held out her left hand and looked down at the little green frond trapped in clear stone. 'It might not be valuable in money terms, but it's very precious to me. I wouldn't swap it for all the ordinary old diamond rings in the world!'

'Oh.'

So Andrew was right.

'But wouldn't you like a sparkly necklace or earrings as well as your own ring? You'd look so beautiful!'

Mum made a funny face. 'Am I so dull to look at now?'

'No! That's not what I meant. I just thought it would be nice for special times.'

'It's a kind thought, Izz, but I can't be doing with jewels. They cost so much and then you have to worry about them being stolen. And, after all, they're only small, hard stones.'

'I was going to get you bulbs for the garden before the bumph thing arrived.'

'Now you're talking! I'd like that very much – some real, living beauty.'

So Izzy told her mother about the bulb plan that would write a special message across the lawn.

'That would take a heck of a lot of bulbs,' said Mum. 'And it would get spoiled if anyone played football when the flowers came up. You do like to think big, don't you, my Izz! A few crocuses would be quite enough. I would love having them to look forward to in the spring.'

'I've got some money still.'

'That's settled then. Come on, let's take a

look outside and plan where my birthday bulbs will go.'

'Now? In the dark?'

'It's not really dark – look! The sun's on its way. Come on, Izz. Pull on a coat and let's watch our birthday dawn!'

Izzy took Dad's big gardening coat and slipped her feet into his huge wellington boots. Then she walked out into the chill, damp air of morning. The sky was pink and gold behind black silhouetted trees. Mum pointed.

'Look at that, Izz. Fairy diamonds!'

The lawn sparkled. It was covered in a delicate lacework of silver threads that bounced and quivered. All along the threads clung droplets of dew that glinted in the pink morning light.

'It's nothing to do with fairies,' said Izzy. She was giving up fairies along with lies and wishes and everything else like that. 'It's wet spiders' webs.'

'I know, I know,' said Mum. 'It's gossamer. But isn't it magical? Isn't it more lovely than any gemstone you could ever buy?'

'It won't last.'

'Of course it won't. That's the beauty of it! It can't be taken and trapped in the claws of any ring. Nobody could ever take it and sell it.'

Mum stood behind Izzy and held her tight, her chin resting on the top of Izzy's head. 'This is a real birthday treat, Izz. To be here with you now and seeing this!'

'Do you believe in magic, Mum?'

'On mornings like this I do!'

'If you could have anything you wanted, what would you ask for?'

Mum thought for a moment. 'I'm very happy with what I've got really. Perhaps a bit more time and . . .'

' . . . Peace!' laughed Izzy. 'I know!'

'What do you want, my Izz? What do you dream of?'

Izzy looked at the sparkling gossamer. 'I'd like a silver flute and I'd like to wear a dress the colour of that sky and jewels like those spiders' webs, and I would play my flute all round the world and . . .'

A tapping noise on the patio door made Izzy and her mother turn around. A small, pink pig looked up at them. It was Grace with her face squashed tight against the glass. Mum pulled the door open.

'And what do you want most in the whole world, you disGrace?' she asked.

'Dit-dit,' said Grace.